LANDFORMS

Written by Teresa Turner

STECK-VAUGHN

A Harcourt Company

www.steck-vaughn.com

CONTENTS

CHAPTER 1
WHAT ARE LANDFORMS?

In photographs taken from space, Earth looks like a smooth ball. That's because the photographs are taken from far away. Up close, however, Earth looks anything but smooth. The top of Mount Everest, the highest point on Earth, reaches $5\frac{1}{2}$ miles (8.8 kilometers) into the sky. Earth's lowest point, the Mariana Trench in the Pacific Ocean, sinks 7 miles (11 kilometers) below the sea. Earth's landforms range from towering mountains to deep canyons and caves. Each type of landform is different—and beautiful.

Earth has several different kinds of **landforms**, but only two processes have created them. In the first process, the large plates of Earth's crust crash together or pull apart. In these places **magma** from the inside of Earth rises through the crust and cools into rock. The second process that has created Earth's landforms is **erosion**. Erosion is the wearing away of rock and soil.

Over thousands of years, wind, water, and ice can shape and even destroy the hardest rock.

The landforms we see every day seem unmoving and permanent. When we look at a mountain, it's hard to believe that it's slowly shrinking. Yet the processes that created our current landforms are still at work. The plates of Earth's crust are sliding under our feet, rivers are digging valleys and canyons, and weather is smoothing mountains and wearing them away.

Because the processes that make landforms often happen slowly, we may not see much change during our lifetime. If we could watch Earth's surface for a million years or so, we would see that it is in constant motion. Blocks of rock are heaved up, sculpted into fantastic shapes, then blown away. **Glaciers** slide down mountains to the sea, leaving long, deep trenches. Seas dry up, then fill again.

As the ground below their feet changes, Earth's creatures have to change, too. Animals **adapt** in many ways. Some change in color. Others develop bodies suited to their environment.

We may not be able to see the birth of a mountain or watch a kind of animal slowly change in color. We

A glacier slowly moving
from land to sea

may not be able to see people learn how to live on
barren **mesas**. However, we can learn about the changes
that have happened to Earth and its creatures. We can
learn how landforms came to be, what is happening to
them now, and the many ways that animals and people
have adapted to Earth's changing landforms.

NORTH AMERICA

New Quebec Crater

Quebec Crater

Sogne F

Rocky Mountains

Teton Range

Laurentian Mountains

Columbia Plateau

Devils Tower

Lascaux Cav

Altamira Cave

Catskill Range

Colorado River

Grand Canyon

Appalachian Mountains

Mammoth Cave

Mississippi River Valley

Atlantic Ocean

S

Pacific Ocean

SOUTH AMERICA

Andes Mountains

N

```
0        1000      2000 Miles
0    1000   2000 Kilometers
Scale at the Equator
```

ASIA

Himalaya
Mountains

Mt. Fuji

*Pacific
Ocean*

Mt. Everest

Mariana
Trench

PE

Nile River

A

Mt. Kenya

Mt. Kilimanjaro

Victoria Falls

ezi
er

*Indian
Ocean*

Key

Desert

Mountains

Plateau

Rift

River

Trench

AUSTRALIA
■ Ayers Rock

ANTARCTICA

7

CHAPTER 2
MOUNTAINS

Mountains tower above the land around them. The sides of some mountains drop almost straight down like huge stone walls, while other mountains slope gently. Some mountains are only as tall as hills, while the **summits** of other mountains reach into the clouds. Some mountains even form on the ocean floor.

Mountain landforms look as though they have been on Earth forever. Some of the world's most spectacular mountains are young, even though they appear to be old. As soon as a mountain is formed, erosion begins to wear it down. Wind, rain, and ice wear away the rock. Most older mountain systems, such as the Laurentians (luh REN shuhnz) in Canada, are low and smooth because they have been worn down over millions and millions of years. Younger mountain systems, such as the Rocky Mountains in North America, are tall and jagged.

Mountains are formed in several ways. Volcanoes form some mountains by piling up mounds of lava. Volcanoes form in places where Earth's crust splits. The split is called a **fault**. Magma spews up through the fault. Magma that has been ejected by a volcano is called lava. The lava piles up around the volcano. After it cools, it becomes rock. The result is a cone- or dome-shaped mountain. Japan's Mount Fuji was made by a volcano.

Folded mountain ranges actually start out as small valleys in Earth's **mantle**. The mantle is the layer of ground between the crust and the center of Earth.

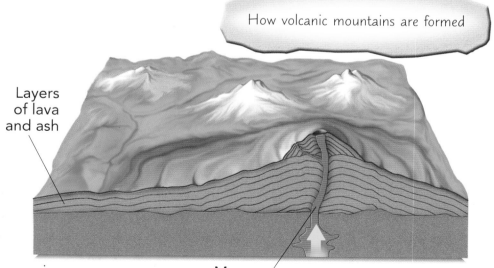

How volcanic mountains are formed

Layers of lava and ash

Magma

These low places then fill with material. Crust plates push in on the material, slowly turning it into rock and folding it. Folded mountains have ridges and valleys that all run in the same direction. The Appalachian (ap uh LAY chuhn) Mountains are an example of folded mountains. When the crust plates run into each other, one plate is sometimes pushed above the other, creating mountains such as the Himalayas of Tibet and India.

Sometimes a large slab of rock is pushed upward. The result is a block mountain. One edge of the slab is usually pushed up farther than the other. The Tetons (TEE tahns) in Wyoming are block mountains.

Another kind of mountain starts out as an underground lake of magma. As the magma cools

How folded mountains are formed

Layers of rock

and is pushed up, it pushes the rock on top of it into a dome shape. Eventually this top layer of rock wears away and shows **granite** beneath. The Andes (AN deez) Mountains in South America were formed in this way.

Erosion creates some types of mountains. These mountains start out as broad, tall masses of land. Wind and water erode these masses and create mountains. The Catskill Mountains in New York were made by erosion.

The Rocky Mountains stretch 3000 miles (4800 kilometers) from Canada to New Mexico. The Rockies contain all sorts of mountains. This mountain system includes folded mountains, block mountains, volcanic mountains, and other types of mountains.

After mountains form, erosion begins to wear them away. Some mountains erode more slowly than others. The Himalayas are made of extremely hard rock that has been pushed up high above Earth's surface. Because this rock resists erosion, these mountains can stand tall for a long time.

Erosion sometimes leaves behind **monoliths**. Perhaps the most famous monolith is Ayers Rock in Australia. This huge sandstone rock is 1100 feet (335 meters) tall and just over 2 miles (3.6 kilometers) long.

Another giant monolith of rock is Devils Tower in Wyoming. The sides of this rock soar 867 feet (264 meters) above the plain. Erosion has left long ridges down its sides.

Strangely enough, scientists think it's possible that Devils Tower was formed under the ground. They think magma may have risen up through Earth's crust and then hardened into a solid pillar. The softer ground could have gradually eroded and uncovered the hard pillar.

Devils Tower in Wyoming

Before Europeans came to the southwestern United States, the Kiowa (KY uh wuh) and Cheyenne (shy EHN) American Indians invented a story to explain how Devils Tower was formed. In their story a giant bear was chasing their people. They called on the earth to help them, and the rock under their feet rose into the air. Trying to reach them, the giant bear clawed at the rock and left long, deep scratches.

From the ground, Devils Tower looks completely bare, but a few plants and animals manage to live on its top. Climbers who have been among the grasses, sagebrush, and prickly pear have seen snakes, wood mice, and chipmunks.

A mountain is a world all its own. Mountains often have plants and animals that are different from those of the land around them. Mountains even have their own climate, which can be very different from the climate of the surrounding area. High up on a mountain, the air is cool and thin. The thin atmosphere doesn't trap much heat. When the sun goes down, the temperature drops even more.

At a certain height, a mountain's climate becomes very cold and windy. Trees cannot grow above this height.

The tree line on a mountain in Canada

This height is called the tree line, and it is visible from far away. A mountain has lots of growth below the tree line and almost no growth above. Only hardy grasses and shrubs can live above the tree line.

The high mountains are beautiful, but life there can be difficult. Most people are happy to live on less harsh land. Still, a few groups of people, such as those of the Andes Mountains and the Himalayas, have learned to live on the mountain tops. Not surprisingly, these people have developed similar ways of life.

Some people of the Andes Mountains in South America live about 12,000 feet (3600 meters) above sea level. A large lake on one high plain provides water to grow grains and potatoes. Nothing but tough grasses grows on other high plains. The people who live there raise sheep, llamas, and alpacas. They have raised these animals for more than 4000 years. Although most people would get sick if they tried to live at such a high **altitude**, the people of the Andes have adapted to the height and the extreme cold.

Llamas and alpacas in the Andes provide wool for warm clothing.

On Chang Thang, a high plain in the Himalaya Mountains, temperatures are fierce. A winter night can be well below freezing. Like the people of the Andes, the Tibetans who live on Chang Thang raise animals— mostly sheep, goats, and yaks that graze on the grasses. Because the grasses are sparse, the Tibetans must move their herds often. The people of Chang Thang follow their herds, carrying their yak's-hair tents to protect them from the cold of their mountain home.

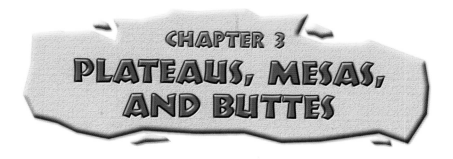

CHAPTER 3
PLATEAUS, MESAS, AND BUTTES

A **plateau** may be the most difficult landform to see because it is big, high, and flat. Some plateaus cover thousands of square miles. Some contain mountain ranges. Streams and rivers cut deeply into most plateaus.

Almost half of Earth's surface is covered by plateaus. The largest plateaus are made of huge slabs of rock that were pushed above the ground. Some smaller plateaus were formed when lava flowed out of deep cracks in the ground and spread over a wide area, burying any mountains in its path. The Columbia Plateau in the northwestern United States was formed by lava flows.

Plateaus made of hard rock have steep sides. Rivers or streams that flow over these plateaus form waterfalls. At Victoria Falls in Africa, the Zambezi River plunges 355 feet (108 meters) down the side of a plateau.

Victoria Falls in Africa

Because of the mist that hangs over Victoria Falls, local people call this place "the smoke that thunders."

Mesas are flat like plateaus, but they are much smaller. Mesas are carved out by the wind in dry landscapes where there are few plants to hold the rock and soil in place. Some mesas are made of harder rock than the rock that once surrounded them. Other mesas are made of softer rock topped with a layer of very hard rock. As erosion eats away at a mesa, the mesa eventually becomes a **butte**.

Most mesas are barren places, but the Hopi people of the southwestern United States have made their homes on mesas for hundreds of years. The Hopi live in mud brick "apartment houses" called pueblos.

Crops will not grow on the tops of the mesas, so the Hopi must farm fields on the plains below. They choose places where rainwater collects and water their fields to make up for the lack of rain. The fields are often many miles away from the mesa. Today some Hopi still live on the mesas where their ancestors settled.

A pueblo on top of a New Mexico mesa

CHAPTER 4
DUNES

Pale golden hills stretch all the way to the horizon. Footprints sink into the soft sand and then disappear in the wind. These landforms can seem like those of another planet, but they are dune landforms in a desert.

Dunes are rare landforms. They cover a very small part of the world's desert area. Most dunes are found in the Middle East and northern Africa.

The shapes that dunes take depend on the direction and speed of the wind. Head dunes form when wind blows sand against an object, such as a rock or a small bush. The sand piles up in front of the object, and soon the object is buried in a dune. A head dune has a steep side toward the wind and a gentle slope away from the wind. During a sandstorm, a head dune can pile up around any still object, even a resting camel!

In some deserts the wind usually blows in one direction. At the edge of these deserts, the wind forms small U-shaped dunes. These are called barchan dunes. The ends of the U point away from the wind. As the wind blows, it pushes sand grains up one side of the dune and over its crest. Then the sand grains roll down the other slope. In this way the whole dune creeps forward as fast as 50 feet (15 meters) in a year!

Seif (SAYF) dunes form deep inside a desert. These large, long dunes are ridges of sand formed by the wind. They can grow to be 130 feet (40 meters) high and 2000 feet (600 meters) wide. Sand that slips down the sides of the dunes is picked up by the wind and blown back onto the dune.

In places where the wind blows in two different directions, seif dunes and barchan dunes may combine to make a surface that looks like waves on the ocean. These places are called sand seas.

Sand dunes of Death Valley in California

Lizards and snakes are found on or near sand dunes because of the warm temperatures that they need. Two types of lizards have developed special feet that keep them from sinking into the sand. One type has webs of skin between its toes, while another type has toes with feathery fringes.

Many types of lizards burrow under the sand. Some do this to escape predators. Others burrow to stay out of the extreme heat. Some lizards "swim" through the sand, looking for insects that live below the surface.

Even though sand dunes have some animal life, they cannot easily support human life. In a hot climate, humans can live for only two days without water. Water helps cool the body. People who haven't drunk enough water die when the temperature goes over 107° F (42° C).

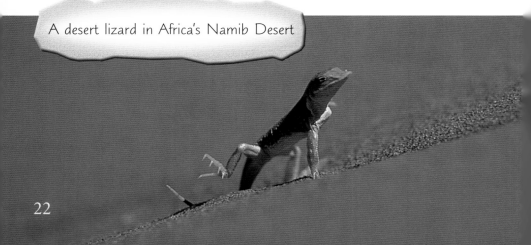

A desert lizard in Africa's Namib Desert

Desert people crossing the Sahara

Although no group of people actually lives on sand dunes, some desert people do travel across them. The Tuareg people of the Sahara Desert are traders who have crossed the desert with camel trains for hundreds of years. Like the Tuareg, the Bedouin people live in tents, wandering the harsh desert dunes with their camels, goats, and sheep.

Desert people stay cool in the heat by wearing long, loose clothing. Their long clothing keeps the burning rays of the sun from reaching their skin. A layer of air trapped between clothing and skin helps keep their body cool.

CHAPTER 5
VALLEYS AND CANYONS

People have lived in river valleys for thousands of years because these valleys often have taller trees and more grassland than the surrounding land. The sides of the valley protect people from wind. The river provides water for crops, as well as fish for food.

The flow of water over thousands of years creates a valley. Where soft and hard rock are mixed, the water wears away the softer rock first. Where the water hits harder rock, it turns aside, bending the river's course as it shapes the valley. Where a river flows through layers of hard rock, the sides of the valley are steep.

Valleys have been very important in human history. One of the greatest **civilizations** in ancient Egypt started in the valley of the Nile River. The Nile flowed through dry land. Every year the rainfall would fill the Nile, which then flooded this dry land. The early Egyptians were able to grow crops once they learned to dig out places to hold the floodwaters. They also built dams around their villages to protect them from the flooding Nile.

The Mississippi River Valley of North America curves and loops through 2350 miles (3781 kilometers) of land. The valley has long been a center of civilization. When pioneers reached the Mississippi, they built farms and towns on its banks. Over thousands of years, the Mississippi River has swept dirt down from the northern states to build a rich **delta**.

The Mississippi River

In 1927 people found out that the big river could be dangerous. In that year the Mississippi overflowed its banks and flooded 23,000 square miles (59,570 square kilometers) of land. Whole towns lay underwater. After this flood, the United States government built structures to keep the Mississippi River within its banks. Concrete **levees** were built along most of its length. **Reservoirs** to hold floodwaters were also built. These changes made life near the river a little safer, but they did not entirely tame the Mississippi. It flooded again in 1973 and 1993.

Not all rivers and streams create their own valleys. Sometimes they take over a valley that is already there. When two plates of Earth's crust move apart from each other, they leave a **rift valley**. One of our planet's largest rift valleys is the Great Rift Valley. It starts in Asia and continues for 3976 miles (6400 kilometers) into eastern Africa. The system of rifts that make up the Great Rift Valley also produced many volcanoes. Mount Kilimanjaro and Mount Kenya were both formed by volcanoes in the East African Rift System. This rift system is part of the Great Rift Valley.

Deep, square-bottomed valleys with steep sides are called canyons. Most canyons are found in dry places.

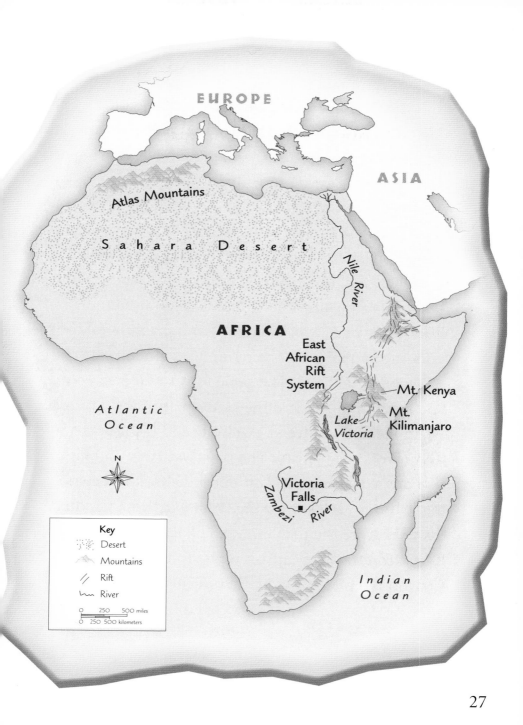

EUROPE

ASIA

Atlas Mountains

S a h a r a D e s e r t

Nile River

AFRICA

East
African
Rift
System

Mt. Kenya

Lake
Victoria

Mt.
Kilimanjaro

Atlantic
Ocean

N

Victoria
Falls

Zambezi River

Indian
Ocean

Key

Desert

Mountains

Rift

River

0   250   500 miles

0   250 500 kilometers

Long ago, a river began the process of digging a canyon. When the rock on either side of the river was exposed, wind and weather made the rock crumble, causing the bottom of the canyon to widen.

One of the world's most awesome sights is the Grand Canyon in northern Arizona. It is 227 miles (446 kilometers) long, 18 miles (29 kilometers) wide, and 6000 feet (1800 meters) deep at its deepest point. The area that is now the Grand Canyon used to be flat millions of years ago. Then heat and pressure folded the land into mountains. The mountains eroded, and the sea flooded the land. The same forces that created the Rocky Mountains lifted the land up, forming a plateau.

Six million years ago, the Colorado River began to flow across the plateau. The river was large and fast. It also carried a huge amount of mud, sand, and gravel that cut out what is now the Grand Canyon. Gradually the river wore the rock away, and landslides tore away large chunks of the canyon walls. Today the Grand Canyon is a place of incredible beauty.

Arizona's Grand Canyon

Glaciers usually do not make their own valley. Instead, they use valleys already formed by streams or rivers. However, glaciers greatly change these valleys by straightening them or shaping them.

Earth contains many landforms created by glaciers. Where glaciers once joined the ocean, they left **fiords**, or steep valleys filled by the sea. One of the world's largest fiords is Sogne (SOHN yuh) Fiord in Norway. It reaches 120 miles (74.5 kilometers) inland. Its deepest point is several miles deep, and its walls tower several thousand feet above the water.

A fiord in New Zealand

CHAPTER 6
CRATERS AND CAVES

Most landforms are created gradually. They form over thousands or millions of years. Some, however, appear with a bang! Throughout Earth's history, **meteorites** have raced through the sky and slammed into our planet. They have left behind huge round holes called **craters**.

When a meteorite crashes into Earth, it sends powerful shock waves deep into the ground. These shock waves bounce back into the meteorite, which then explodes. A meteorite impact can release as much energy as a nuclear bomb! This energy melts the meteorite. It becomes small glassy balls. The largest crater that scientists have studied is the New Quebec Crater in Quebec, Canada. It has a diameter of 11,000 feet (3352 meters) and a depth of 1300 feet (396 meters).

A crater created by a meteor in Arizona

Unlike craters, most cave landforms form very slowly and go through four stages. In the first stage, water seeps into cracks in the ground. At first these cracks are tiny. It takes at least 3000 years for the water to widen a crack to the size of a pencil. Once the crack widens, the water gains speed. It carries acid that helps it erode the rock.

In the second stage, the crack grows more rapidly. In about 10,000 years, a young cave may only grow a few yards or meters in width. When the water stops flowing or finds another path, the cave enters the third stage of its life, where not much change occurs. This stage can last a very long time. The fourth stage of cave life is decay. As the ground changes around a cave, a cave's rooms are cut into smaller rooms, or they simply fall down. Many caves have very long lifetimes. Mammoth Cave in Kentucky has some passages that are 2 million years old!

How does dripping rainwater wear away solid rock? The answer is in the minerals that make up the rock. When rainfall hits the ground, it picks up small amounts of carbon dioxide and forms a weak, fizzy acid that dissolves the minerals found in the rocks. The water picks up more carbon dioxide as it travels through the ground and seeps through cracks and holes in rock. The acid becomes stronger and starts to dissolve the rock. As it does so, caves are formed underground.

Some caves have underground streams. Many caves have more than one level and many passages. Mammoth Cave is the longest cave in the world. It has six levels and more than 300 miles (482 meters) of passages. Mammoth Cave even has underground lakes and rivers as well as many beautiful rock formations. Many caves also have strange natural decorations inside them.

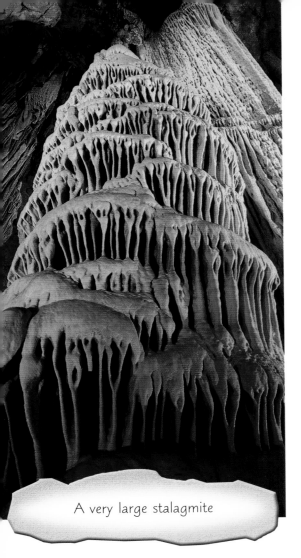

A very large stalagmite

While the water seeps through the ground and picks up carbon dioxide, some of this water drips from a cave's ceiling. The water and tiny bits of the dissolved stone harden into long, icicle-shaped **stalactites**. When the water drips down from the tip of a stalactite, it deposits more rock on the cave's floor. This rock forms a **stalagmite** directly underneath the stalactite.

A stalactite and a stalagmite sometimes build up so much over time that they form a column from ceiling to floor. When a sheet of water flows down a sloping cave ceiling, it makes **flowstone**. Flowstone looks like cloth drapes.

Caves can also form in lava. Sometimes, when the outer layer of a lava flow cools and hardens, the hot lava inside keeps flowing. The cool crust stays behind while the lava inside drains away, forming a long tube. These tubes can be hundreds of yards or meters long. Sometimes strong-flowing lava breaks the hardened crust above it, causing it to buckle and rise up like a tent. A small cave is left beneath the tent.

Caves are nature's houses. Because they offer protection from the weather, many kinds of animals live in or seek shelter in caves. Of course, the best-known animals that live in caves are bats. Some animals, like bears, use caves as a place to sleep in winter.

Early people were drawn to caves. There they left some of the earliest artwork. Millions of years ago, people used clay and charcoal to paint pictures in caves. They also carved pictures into the rock. Most cave drawings show animals. Some of these animals are now extinct.

Altamira, a cave in northern Spain, has some of the most famous cave paintings. This cave contains nearly life-size paintings of buffalo. Another cave famous for its artwork is Lascaux (las KOH) Cave in France.

Animals carved into a
cave wall long ago

The colors of the paintings in this cave are still bright.
One picture in the Lascaux cave shows a group of deer
swimming across a river.

In addition to paintings of animals, many caves
contain outlines of human hands. No one knows why
early people made these handprints. They remain as a
record of some of our earliest ancestors.

GLOSSARY

adapt (uh DAPT) to change to fit a different environment

altitude (AL tih tood) height above sea level

butte (byoot) a steep hill with a flat top

civilizations (siv uh luh ZAY shuhnz) cultures and societies developed by groups of people or countries

craters (KRAY tuhrz) large holes shaped like bowls

delta (DEL tuh) a triangle-shaped piece of land at the mouth of a river

erosion (ih ROH zhuhn) a gradual wearing away by the action of water, wind, or ice

fault (fawlt) a split in Earth's crust

fiords (fyawrdz) long, narrow valleys filled by the sea

flowstone (FLOH stohn) a cave formation made by flowing water

glaciers (GLAY shuhrz) huge masses of ice and snow

granite (GRAN it) a common coarse rock used in monuments and buildings

landforms (LAND fawrmz) shapes that make up Earth's surface

levees (LEV eez) raised banks of ground made to keep rivers from overflowing

magma (MAG muh) melted rock below Earth's surface

mantle (MAN tuhl) the layer of ground below Earth's crust

mesas (MAY suhz) mountains with steep sides and flat tops

meteorites (MEE tee uhr ites) stone or metal objects that have fallen to Earth from outer space

monoliths (MAHN uh lihths) very large stones

plateau (pla TOH) a large piece of high, flat land

reservoirs (REZ uhr vwahrz) manmade lakes

rift valley (rift VAL eez) a valley created by the movement of plates that form Earth's crust

stalactites (stuh LAK tyts) icicle-shaped stones hanging from the roof of a cave

stalagmite (stuh LAG myts) a stone rising up from the floor of a cave

summits (SUH mihtz) the highest points of mountains

INDEX